First published 1993 by Walker Books Ltd
87 Vauxhall Walk, London SE11 5HJ

This edition published 2009

2 4 6 8 10 9 7 5 3 1

The right of Lucy Su to be identified as author/illustrator of this work
has been asserted by her in accordance with the Copyright, Designs and Patents Act 1988

This book has been typeset in Garamond Educational

Printed in China

British Library Cataloguing in Publication Data:
a catalogue record for this book is available from the British Library.

ISBN 978-0-7445-2632-5

www.walker.co.uk

This Little Piggy

Lucy Su

WALKER BOOKS

AND SUBSIDIARIES

LONDON · BOSTON · SYDNEY · AUCKLAND

This little piggy
went to market,

This little piggy
stayed at home,

This little piggy
had roast beef,

This little piggy
had none,

And this little piggy

cried, *wee-wee-wee,*

All the way home.

This little piggy went to market,
This little piggy stayed at home,
This little piggy had roast beef,
This little piggy had none,
And this little piggy cried,
wee-wee-wee,
All the way home.